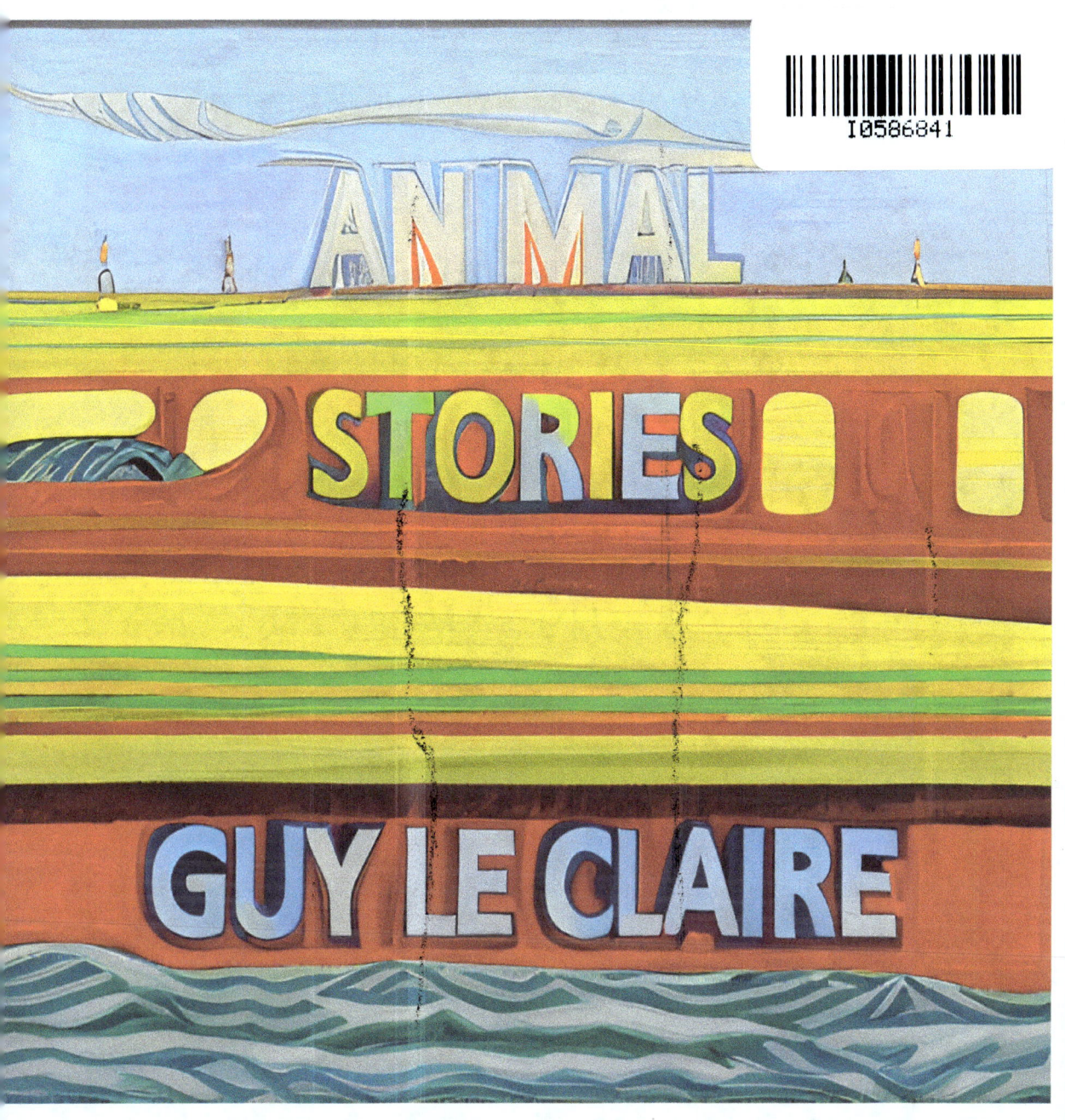

ANIMAL STORIES

GUY LE CLAIRE

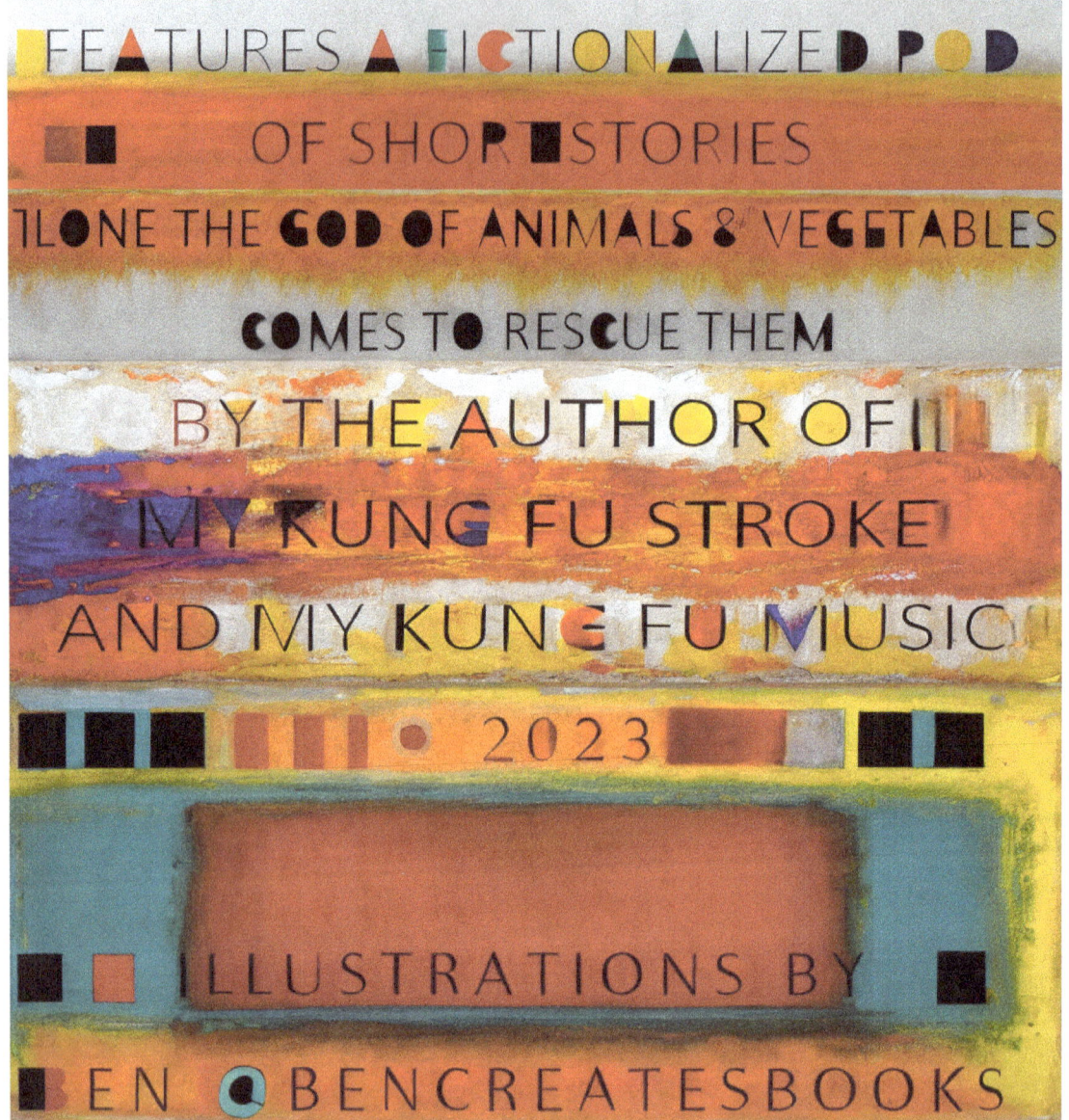

FEATURES A FICTIONALIZED POD

OF SHORT STORIES

1LONE THE GOD OF ANIMALS & VEGETABLES

COMES TO RESCUE THEM

BY THE AUTHOR OF

MY KUNG FU STROKE

AND MY KUNG FU MUSIC

2023

ILLUSTRATIONS BY

BEN @BENCREATESBOOKS

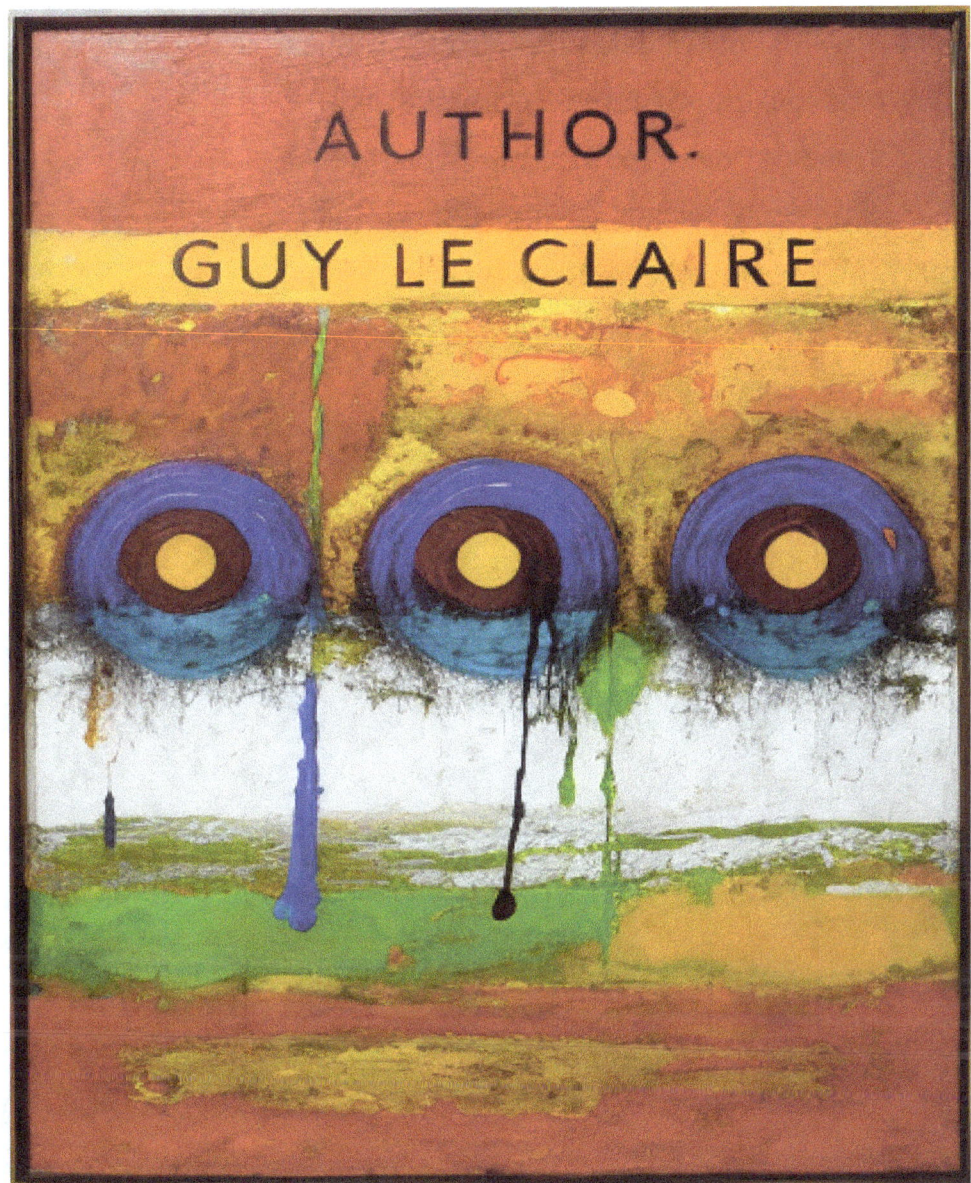

In the beginning All the Animals lined up in the abattoirs, developed a psychic energy and ability, the older ones noticed how when they channeled a thought their tribes were picking up on it. No one had ever made it back to the farm to tell of the insistent human methods,

but, apparently there was a developing
apprehension growing in the humans. As the
younger upcoming slaughter victims developed
these psychic abilities as taught by the
elders, One Day the butchers stopped and
disappeared.

CHARLES

Charles the Causeway Bay cockroach spoke Cantonese with an upper class accent.

However he loved hanging out at the Causeway Bay to Sai Kung mini bus stop, around midnight as there was always a good selection of human spew to wade around in.

But on this particular night. A blokes girlfriend screamed so a Wei stomped on Charlie. There is a plaque there where he died.

ELOISE

Eloise was the prettiest and grandest vegetable stalk in the field. Every morning she raised herself to the sun then bathed in the water sprinkled about her. Lifes Good.

One day she heard a loud machine like noise. I wish I could run she thought. And within a fraction she and all of her mates were chopped to be spewn into a trolley at the machines rear. She had become one of the demographic.

FREDDY

Freddy the funnel Web, decided to spend the night in a round black rubber thing next to his hole in the ground.

By morning, waking to jolts and wind, grumpily, he hopped out only to nd himself at the top of katoomba St, opposite the Carrington. This looks jolly good he said to himself, as he crossed the road a car ran over him. Unt dasvas dee end of das.

Harold the lamb. Sat stunned and began sobbing as the truck he was placed in bumpingly sped off from his Tribe in a whirl of dust. Old jimbo sheep had warned the young ones of their predicament a few days ago. And cautioned them all to be ready to meet sheep god i lone. Harold couldn't believe it. Y is this happening to me!? As all the lambs shat and pissed and cried in this alien spaceshit. A Road train. When Harold met the god ilone. God said and ye shall be served up on the Smiths and Morgans dinner table. Ur sacri ce will be gruntingly appreciated. And in a flash so it came to be.

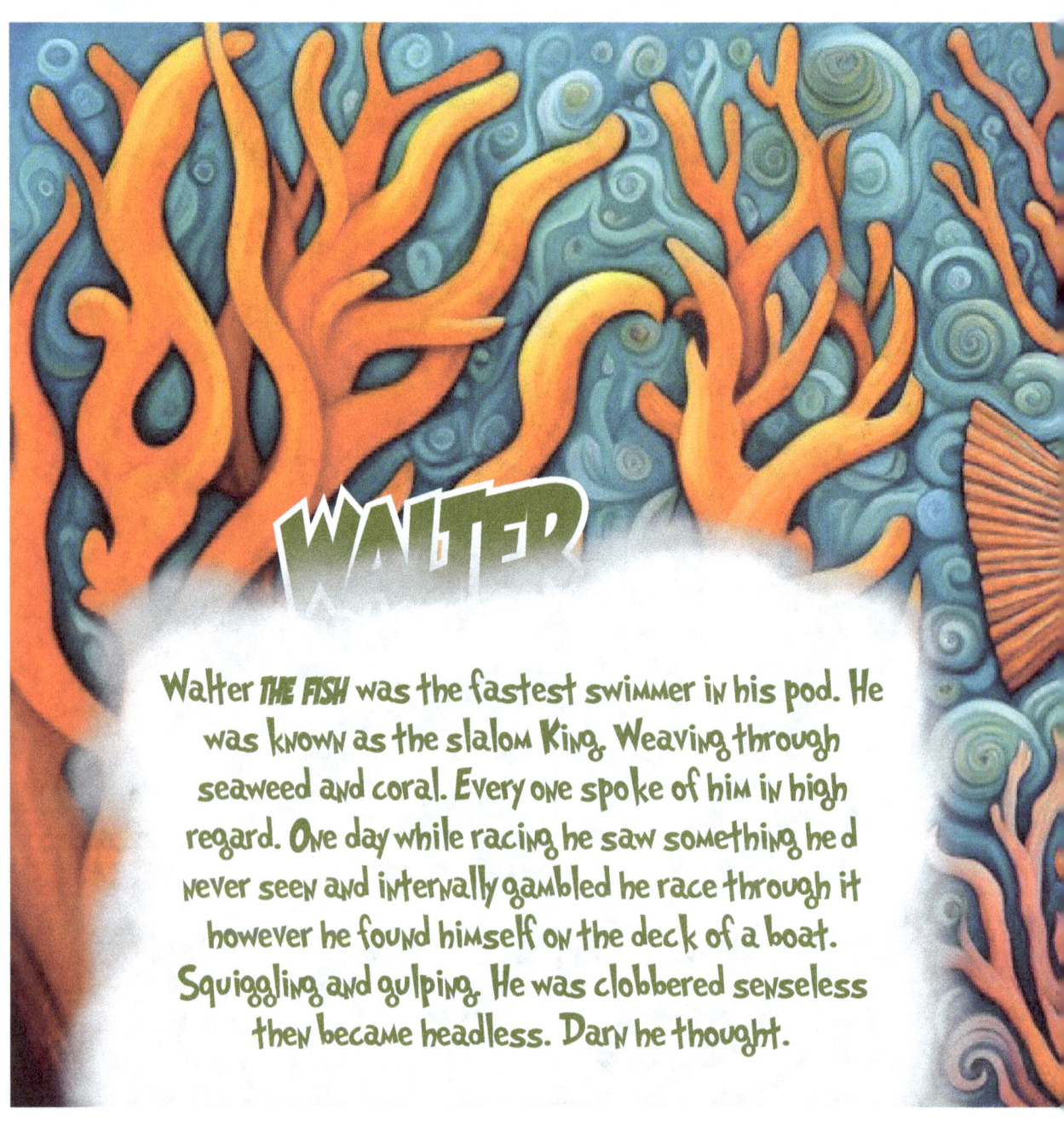

WALTER

Walter *THE FISH* was the fastest swimmer in his pod. He was known as the slalom King, Weaving through seaweed and coral. Every one spoke of him in high regard. One day while racing he saw something he'd never seen and internally gambled he race through it however he found himself on the deck of a boat. Squiggling and gulping. He was clobbered senseless then became headless. Darn he thought.

WANKERICK

Wankerick, from the Human tribe thought he had it all sorted, until one day after posing off, boys in blue took him in, he kicked and lied until those boys locked him up.. no one does this to me he thought especially spazos. Cruising along on his tribal made machine terribly advanced from the flintstone era, a bigger similar thing went straight into him. Unt das vas dee end of das.

ANNIE THE ALIEN

Annie took a bit of a fancy for male rhinoceroses. Harvey Rhino prodded Annie with his horn and Annie flew back to Jupiter.

Tammy the nurse, fancied human rump,
took a bite and ended up speared at Manly beach.

TAMMY

Tavlava the tomayto so ripe,
plump and red, took centre stage in
woolies, but her energy was
dissipating. Tavlava got chucked
in the pot

KARLA

Karla the kangaroo lived in Kanimbla valley, every morning she and her friends munched on fresh dew ridden grass in harmony with the Universe. Mother Kangaroo told her tribe a change was coming as she felt it in her tail. Father Kangaroo a shaman, decided to hold a corroboree that night, the mob sung and danced euphorically without a care in the world.

WILLIE

Willie wombat from **Thredbo**, loved all the attention he got. The humans are a strange lot he muttered, then waffled up the **Thredbo** river back to his family

FRED

Fred the Fish started gaining consciousness.
As the new day dawned, the light trinkets began embedding the sea.

At once he was amazed by the number of beautiful females around him, He had his eyes on Betty

He noticed a large shadow and yelled to everyone   Hide! The fish eater slowly eyed it s prey, all the while Betty & Fred hid in a cave...As they waited and looked at each other for what seemed an eon, Betty started praying as Fred peered above waiting for the all clear, this time a low humming noise was approaching, Fred yelled all clear and they all raced upwards playing gymnast games.

Betty then gave Fred a kiss as they all swam for joy. Suddenly, WHOOSH, everyone including Mary, Peter, Fred, Betty & Paul were caught in some kind of net, reeling them up towards the light source. As they all started jumping about on a Hong Kong shing trawler. Fred wondered Diu, is this what it s all about?

Willy wasn't laid to rest just, laid in his wifes bed, when a bird decided to settle on a branch outside wifes bedroom.

Willy believed he was in a telepathic communication with Woody, when all Woody did was meditate.

Woody shaked the rainwater off his body and flew away. at that moment Willy realised the universe is good and forgave every/body/thing.

Harry de huntsman, found a nice possy on the wall, he began his usual gymnastic routine, when suddenly a spray of mist globules landed on his skin The excruciating pain killed him on the spot. flopping to the floor like Zapata.

Outer space, with all the Alien Spaceships drifting around was becoming overwhelmed with Animal and Vegetable spirits.

Ilone their God appeared before them and stated cmon we're all going to heaven, And they did. Everything was good in the worlds. The Abattoirs and farming shut down and Robots took over everything, forcing the human tribes into Slavery.

THE

END